OVER THE TOP

The Story of a Soldier

Dee Phillips

D1213934

SADDLEBACK
EDUCATIONAL PUBLISHING

Yesterday's Voices

A Dream of America
Gladiator
Holocaust
Over the Top
Pirate
Resistance Fighter
Runaway
Samurai
Tail Gunner
Titanic
Vietnam
Viking

© **Copyright Ruby Tuesday Books Limited 2013**
This edition is published by arrangement with ReadZone Books Limited.

Images courtesy of Getty Images (page 19), public domain, and Shutterstock.

Acknowledgements: With thanks to Lorraine Petersen, Chief Executive of NASEN, for her help in the development and creation of these books.

Copyright ©2014 by Saddleback Educational Publishing
All rights reserved. No part of this book may be reproduced in any form or by any means, electronic or mechanical, including photocopying, recording, scanning, or by any information storage and retrieval system, without the written permission of the publisher. SADDLEBACK EDUCATIONAL PUBLISHING and any associated logos are trademarks and/or registered trademarks of Saddleback Educational Publishing.

ISBN-13: 978-1-62250-875-4
ISBN-10: 1-62250-875-0
eBook: 978-1-63078-010-4

Printed in Malaysia

20 19 18 17 16 2 3 4 5 6

The big guns boom all night.
My head feels like it will explode.
I hate the stink of this place.
I wish I was back in the garden.

OVER THE TOP

The Story of a Soldier

"YOUR COUNTRY NEEDS
YOU"

World War 1 began in the summer of 1914. Britain went to war with Germany.

The men of Britain were asked to fight for their king and country.

Thousands of men signed up.

Many young men wanted to go to the battlefields in France. They thought it would be an adventure.

They could not imagine the horror of the battlefields ...

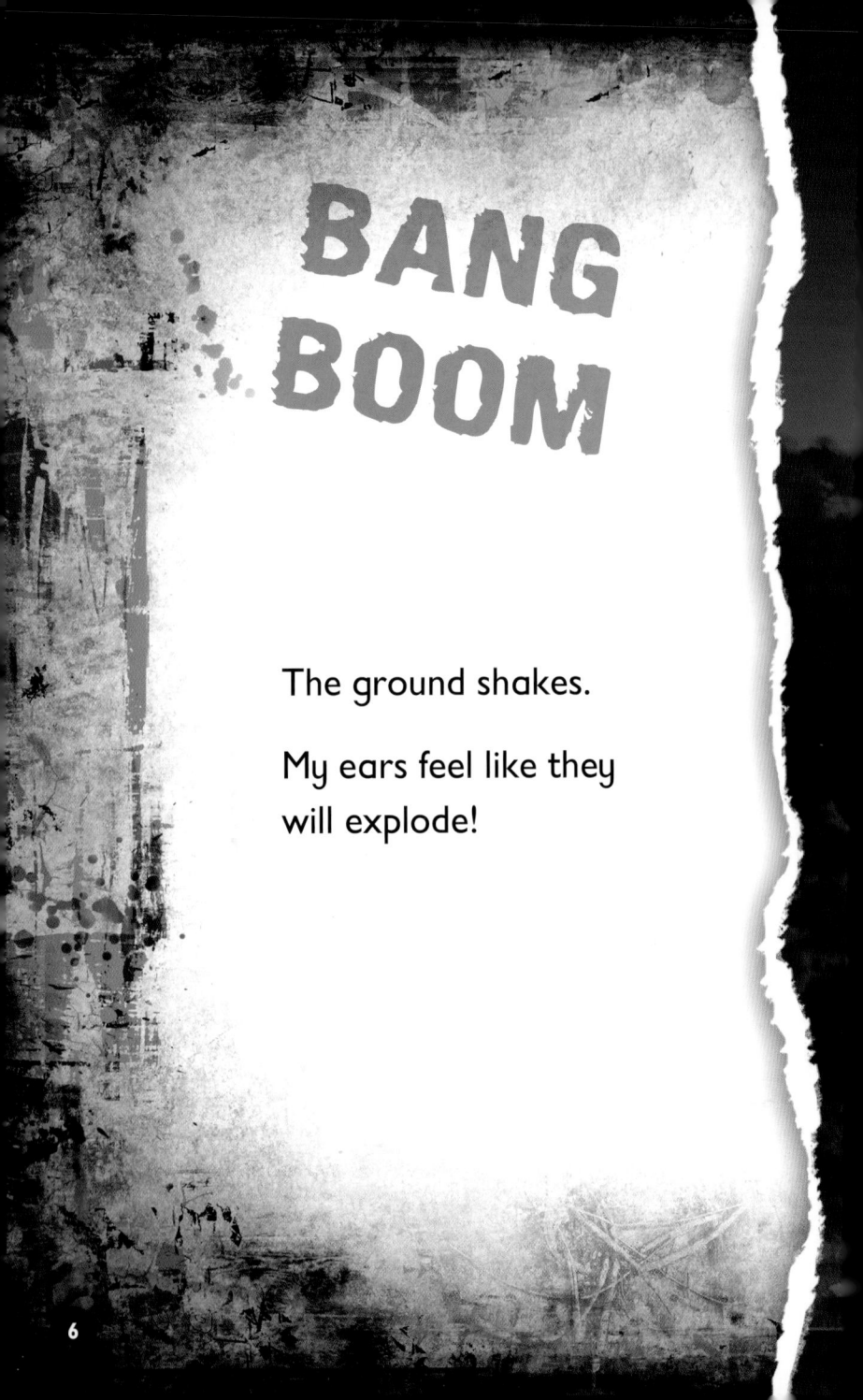

BANG BOOM

The ground shakes.

My ears feel like they will explode!

BANG BOOM

The night sky glows with smoke and fire.
My ears feel like they will explode.

I wish I was back in England.
I wish I was back in the garden.
I wish I could hear a bird sing.

I'm digging.
The sun is warm on my back.
The birds are singing.

I can hear my friend
Harry whistling.
He's planting seeds.

It is cold and wet in the trenches.

My belly rumbles.
We had bread and stew for dinner.
Just one loaf of bread for ten lads.
The bread was hard and dry.
It takes eight days for bread
to get here.

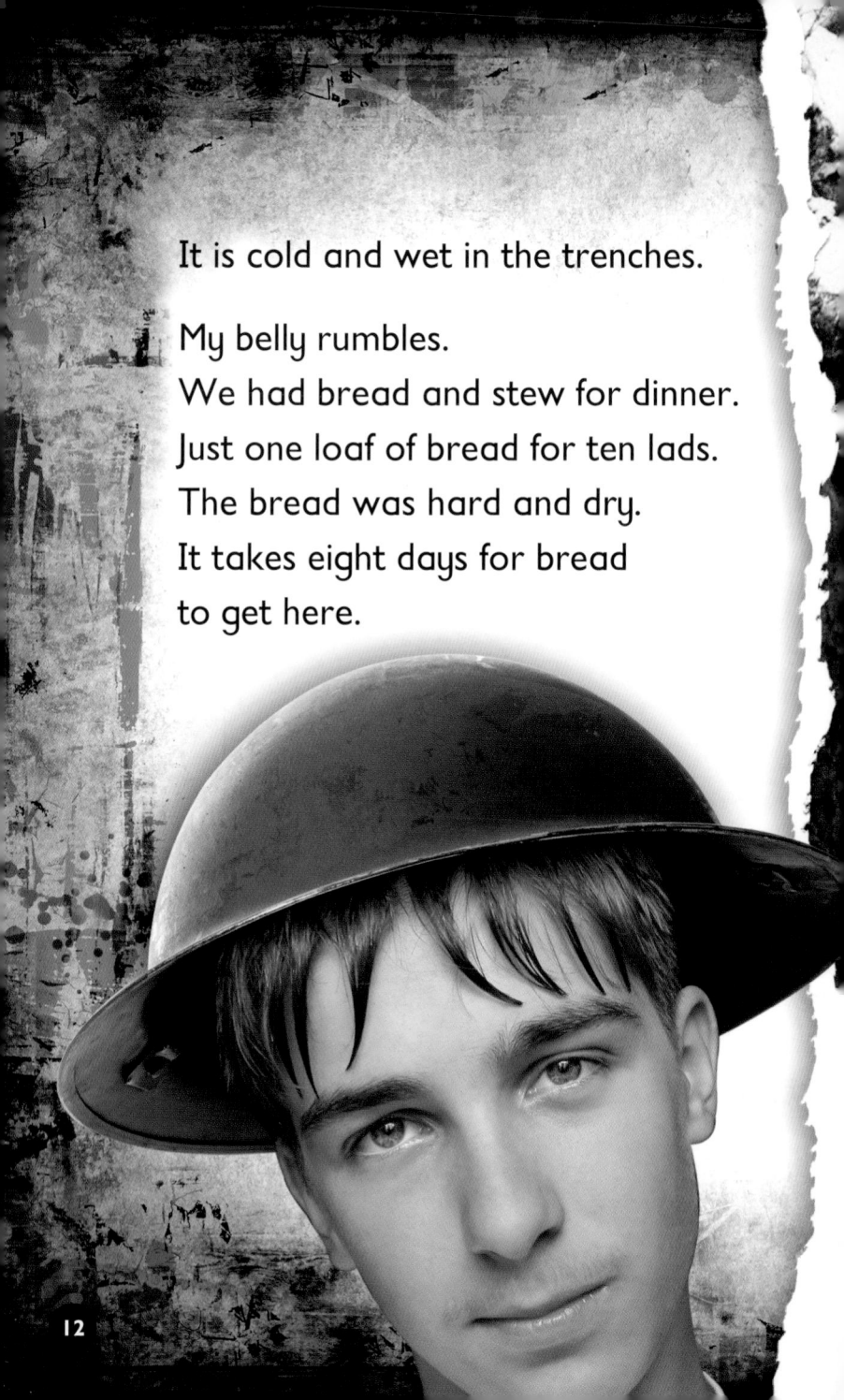

BANG BOOM

There is icy water in the trenches.

Our boots are filled with it
day and night.

Our feet are burning and rotting.

It's trench foot.

All us lads have got it.

Annie
SURELY YOU WILL
FIGHT FOR YOUR
AND
COME ALONG, BOYS,
BEFORE IT IS TOO LATE

We are sitting by the pond.
The sun is hot on my back.
The water is icy cold on my hot feet.

I give Harry half my bread.
It's sweet and soft.
Annie baked it this morning.

Harry says, "I'm going, Jack.
We should go together."

BANG BOOM

I hate the stink of this place.
The stink of our lads rotting
in the mud.

I wish I was back in the garden.

I want to smell flowers
and fruit.

Harry is up high on the ladder.
He's picking apples.
I'm holding the basket.

Harry says, "We'll go on a ship!
Better to be a soldier than a
gardener, Jack."

I love the smell of the apples.

Tonight Annie will bake
apple cake.

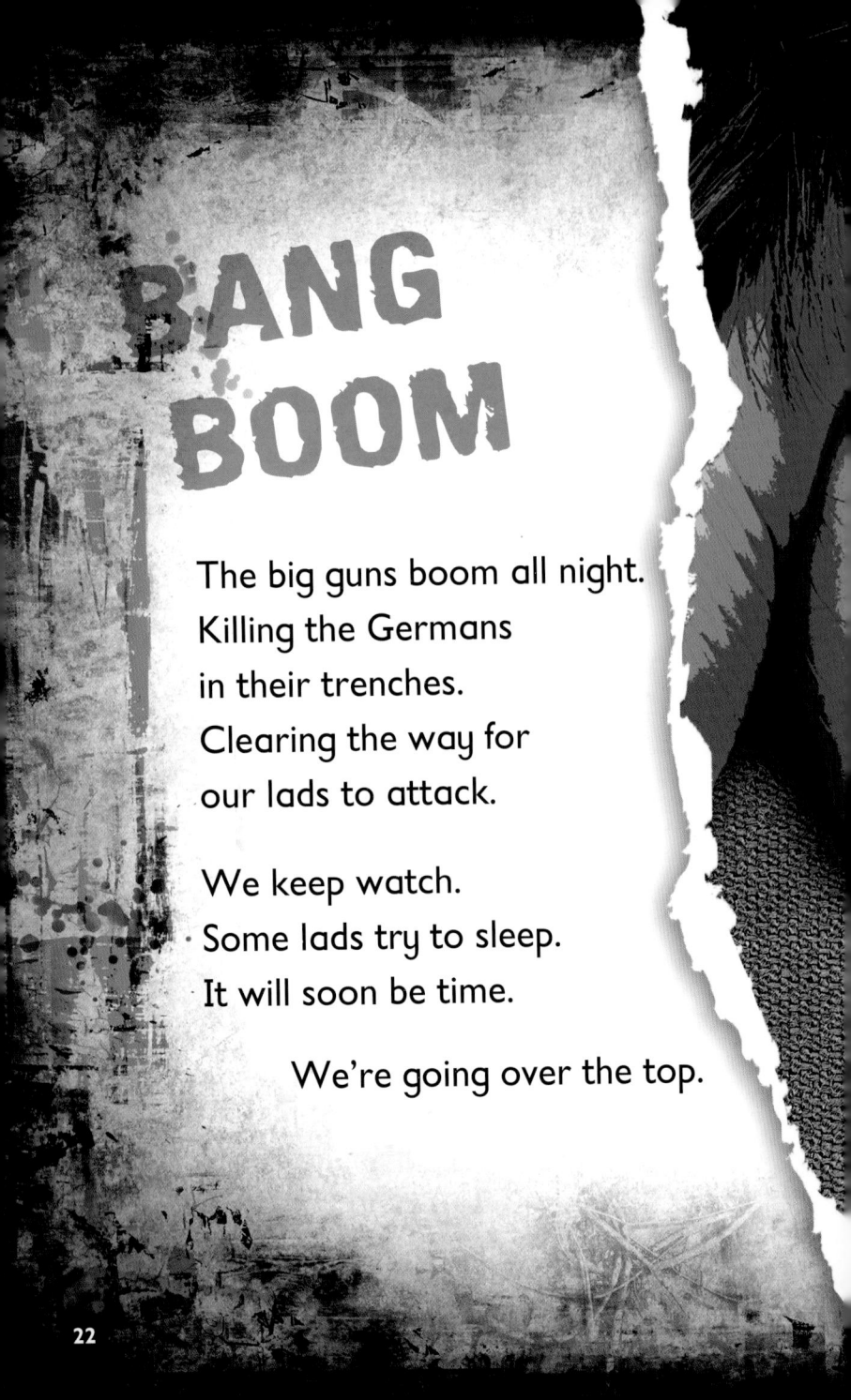

BANG BOOM

The big guns boom all night.
Killing the Germans
in their trenches.
Clearing the way for
our lads to attack.

We keep watch.
Some lads try to sleep.
It will soon be time.

We're going over the top.

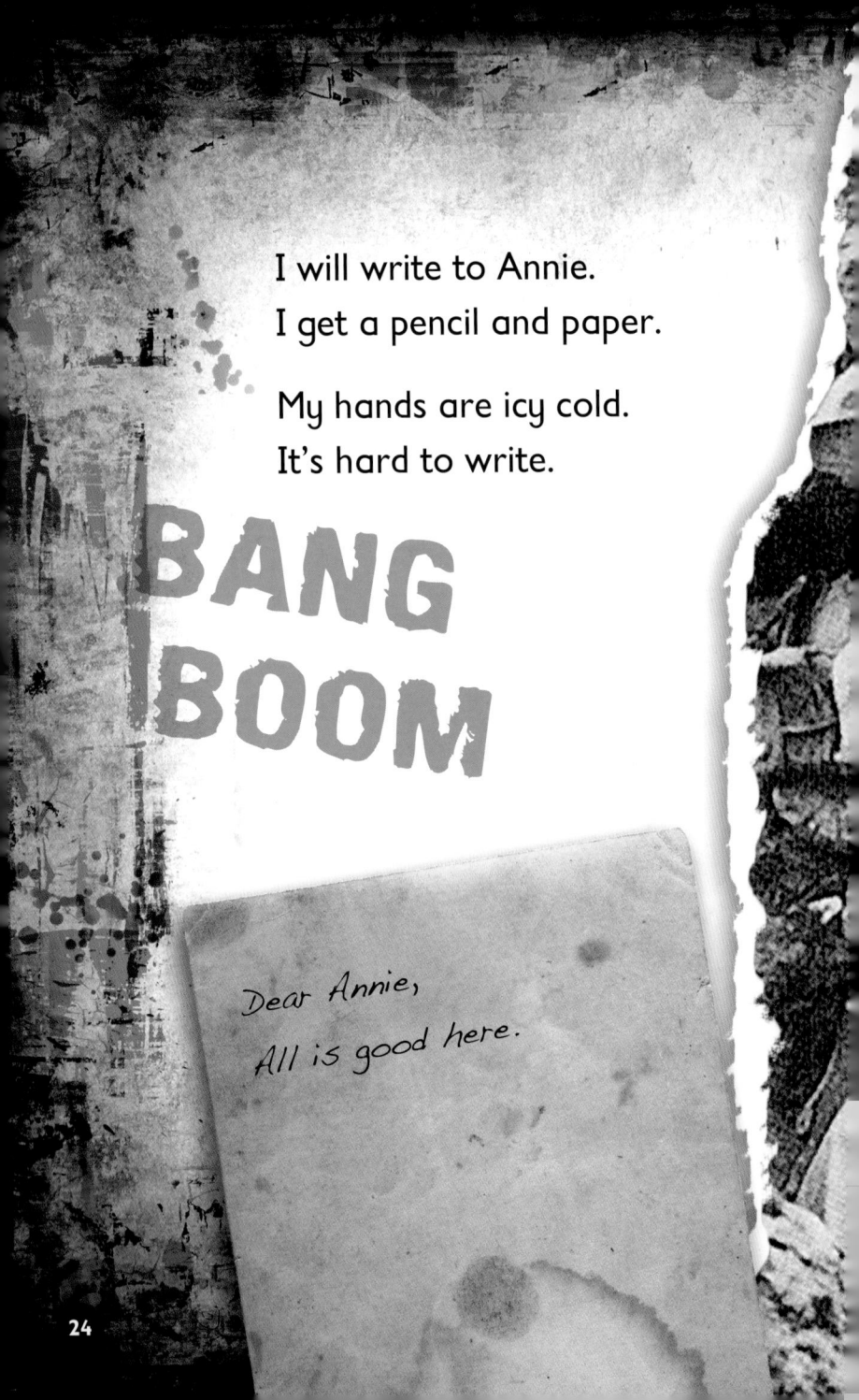

I will write to Annie.
I get a pencil and paper.

My hands are icy cold.
It's hard to write.

BANG
BOOM

Dear Annie,
All is good here.

I open the door.
Harry is there.

Harry says, "Come on, Jack.
We're marching to the coast.
We're off to France, Jack."

Annie tries not to cry.
She says, "Take care,
little brother."

I say, "I'm going to do
my duty, Annie."

Jack
1916
Annie and
Jack 190

BANG BOOM

It's getting light.
It will soon be time.
I stamp my icy, burning feet.
I scratch at the lice in my hair.

My head is filled with pictures.

Sometimes my head feels like it will explode.

I can't forget that night.
Harry was smiling and singing.
The lads were clapping along.

BANG
BANG
BANG

It's getting light.
It will soon be time.
I finish my letter to Annie.
It will be mailed back to England.

The rum is coming around.
A shot of rum for each lad.
A shot of rum to take away the fear.

Then the big guns stop.
It is time.

We are going over the top.

The whistles blow.
I'm climbing out of
the trench.

Running

Deep mud pulls at my boots.
Dead, rotting bodies under
my feet.

Machine
guns
flash

My ears feel like they
will explode.

I have to keep going.

Running and
running.

**Machine
guns
flash**

Sharp wire tears at my legs.

"Better to be a soldier than a gardener, Jack."

Screams all around me.

"Take care, little brother."

I'm doing my duty, Annie.
I have to keep going.

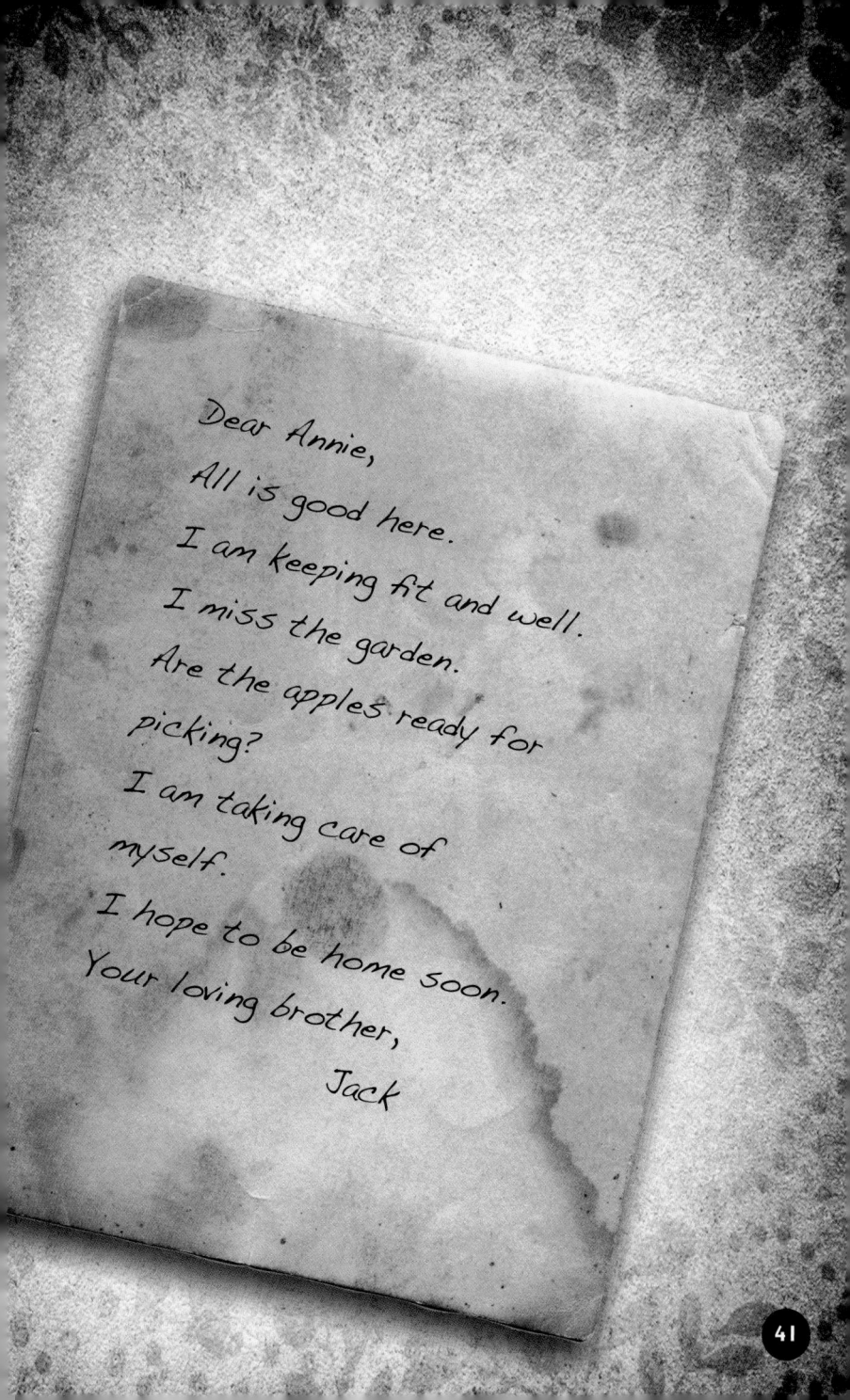

Dear Annie,

All is good here.

I am keeping fit and well.

I miss the garden.

Are the apples ready for picking?

I am taking care of myself.

I hope to be home soon.

Your loving brother,

Jack

OVER THE TOP

Behind the Story

On the battlefields of Europe during the First World War, both sides dug trenches in which soldiers sheltered, fired their weapons, lived, and died.

The trenches were long networks of ditches that armies dug along the front lines of territory they held against the enemy. Soldiers on each side then attacked one another and defended their territory from inside the trenches.

Large weapons, called artillery, provided heavy firepower to support the soldiers in the trenches. These weapons fired large shells and other explosives at enemy positions.

Life in the trenches was miserable, boring, and terrifying. Moments of rest were brief, as enemy artillery attacks could come at any time. These attacks were launched from a great distance away and were impossible to defend against.

Many of the nine million soldiers killed in the First World War died in the trenches. There, artillery, machine-gun fire, and disease made death a constant presence for soldiers on both sides.

Over the Top

Adding to the danger and terror of trench warfare were the times when soldiers went "over the top." Soldiers leapt over the edge of their trench and rushed into an area known as "No Man's Land." Their mission was to cross this area and attack the enemy trenches facing them.

Sometimes this resulted in hand-to-hand combat with enemy soldiers. Often, however, soldiers going over the top were met by a storm of enemy machine-gun fire, leading to a near-certain death.

Soldiers loading large artillery weapons

OVER THE TOP

What's next?

Mom and Dad

Mollie

BACK IN THE GARDEN

ON YOUR OWN / WITH A PARTNER / IN A GROUP

In the story, Jack remembers the garden, the birds singing, the apples, and his sister's cooking. If you were forced to spend time away from your home and everyday life, what would you miss the most?

DEAR ANNIE

ON YOUR OWN

The letter Jack writes to his sister, Annie, does not reveal the full horror of his life in the trenches.

Imagine you are Jack. Write a letter home that tells the truth about the terrible things you are experiencing.

BOOK TALK

IN A GROUP

Jack and Harry are characters in a story. Their story, however, is based on what happened to thousands of men who fought during World War I. Discuss with your group how the story and the facts you've learned about the war make you feel. Think about:

- Could you cope with the conditions that Jack describes in the trenches?
- How do you think the soldiers felt as they went over the top and ran toward the enemy's guns?

A SOLDIER'S SONG

ON YOUR OWN / WITH A PARTNER / IN A GROUP

Many powerful poems and songs have been written about war.

Try writing your own poem or song lyrics about the character Jack or another young soldier in World War I. Think about a theme or main idea for your song. Don't be afraid to write down words or partial ideas—they may give you inspiration later!

I die tomorrow

Hell on earth

the boy from the garden

good-bye home

Titles in the

Yesterday's Voices

series

We jump from our ship and attack. But something feels wrong. I know this place.

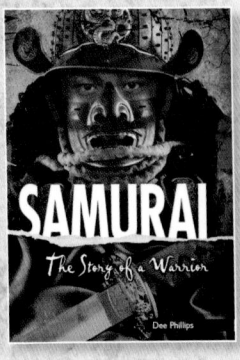

We face each other. Two proud samurai. Revenge burns in my heart.

We saw a treasure ship. Up went our black flag. They could not escape.

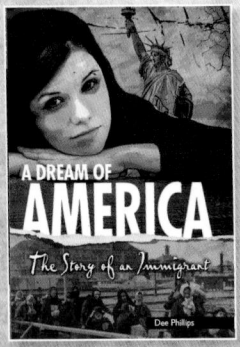

The work is so hard. I miss my home. Will my dream of America come true?

I jumped from the plane. I carried fake papers, a gun and a radio. Now I was Sylvie, a resistance fighter.

Every day we went on patrol. The Vietcong hid in jungles and villages. We had to find them … before they found us.